# HENRY HECKELBECK

## 4 books in 1!

Henry Heckelbeck Gets a Dragon

Henry Heckelbeck Never Cheats

Henry Heckelbeck and the Haunted Hideout

Henry Heckelbeck Spells Trouble

By **Wanda Coven**

Illustrated by **Priscilla Burris**

**LITTLE SIMON**

New York   London   Toronto   Sydney   New Delhi

LITTLE SIMON

An imprint of Simon & Schuster Children's Publishing Division

1230 Avenue of the Americas, New York, New York, 10020

This Little Simon hardcover edition June 2021

*Henry Heckelbeck Gets a Dragon* and *Henry Heckelbeck Never Cheats* copyright © 2019 by Simon & Schuster, Inc. *Henry Heckelbeck and the Haunted Hideout* and *Henry Heckelbeck Spells Trouble* copyright © 2020 by Simon & Schuster, Inc.

LITTLE SIMON is a registered trademark of Simon & Schuster, Inc., and associated colophon is a trademark of Simon & Schuster, Inc. For information about special discounts for bulk purchases, please contact Simon & Schuster Special Sales at 1-866-506-1949 or business@simonandschuster.com. The Simon & Schuster Speakers Bureau can bring authors to your live event. For more information or to book an event contact the Simon & Schuster Speakers Bureau at 1-866-248-3049 or visit our website at www.simonspeakers.com.

Series design by Leslie Mechanic

Manufactured in the United States of America 0521 FFG

10 9 8 7 6 5 4 3 2 1

Library of Congress Control Number 2021936180

ISBN 978-1-6659-0707-1

ISBN 978-1-5344-6105-5 (*Henry Heckelbeck Gets a Dragon* ebook)

ISBN 978-1-5344-6108-6 (*Henry Heckelbeck Never Cheats* ebook)

ISBN 978-1-5344-6118-5 (*Henry Heckelbeck and the Haunted Hideout* ebook)

ISBN 978-1-5344-6121-5 (*Henry Heckelbeck Spells Trouble* ebook)

These titles were previously published individually in hardcover and paperback by Little Simon.

# CONTENTS

# HENRY HECKELBECK

## Gets a Dragon

# ∴ CONTENTS ∴

## Chapter 1

# BACK TO SCHOOL

Henry's eyes popped open.

"First day of school!" he cried. He hopped out of bed, fully dressed.

Henry always slept in his clothes. It saved time.

He brushed his teeth with his special two-sided toothbrush. It could reach every tooth.

Then he zipped into the hallway.

*Blammo!* Henry crashed right into his older sister, Heidi.

"Hey, bub! Watch out next time!" she said.

Henry apologized. "Sorry, sis!"

Then he took off down the stairs. Henry loved his sister, but sometimes she could be a total grump-a-saurus.

Henry slipped into his seat at the table.

Mom gave Henry a strawberry-banana smoothie in a to-go cup. He liked to finish his smoothie on the way to the bus stop. It saved time.

Heidi plunked down at the kitchen table.

"Smoothies?" she complained. "I wanted pancakes."

"Then why don't you turn your smoothie into what you WANT?" Henry suggested.

Heidi looked at Mom.

"No magic at the table,"
Mom said firmly.

Heidi rolled her eyes.

Magic was normal at the
Heckelbeck house.

Heidi was a witch—so were Henry's Mom and Aunt Trudy.

Henry and Dad were regular, everyday people, and Henry was fine with that.

Henry checked the clock and yelled, "Gotta go!"

"Not so fast!" said Dad. "We need a first-day-of-school picture!"

It took a few tries before
they got the best one.

Henry's first day of school
was off to a very normal start.

But today was going to be anything but normal.

That was because Henry Heckelbeck had a secret.

He just didn't know it yet.

## Chapter 2

# BEST BUDS

*Whap! Whap!*

Dudley Day slapped the seat beside him on the bus. Henry and Dudley had been best friends ever since they first met.

"Over here!" Dudley cried, whapping the seat again.

Henry plopped into the spot next to Dudley.

They did their secret handshake, which went like this:

Slap high!

Slap low!

 Slap side to side!

Elbows!

 Fist bump!

Hip bump!

At the end, thumbs-up!

The boys were both in the same class, with a teacher named Ms. Mizzle. She was new to the school this year, so neither one of them had ever met her.

"I wonder what she's like?" asked Dudley.

"I did a little detective work over the summer," Henry said. "I learned a few things about the new teacher, and I took notes."

He flipped open his spy notebook.

"'Real name: Miranda Mizzle. Likes: flowers, gardening, science, math, and wearing yellow hats. Dislikes: kids wiping noses on their sleeves, bullies.'"

Dudley raised his eyebrows. "Where did you get all the info?"

"My mom," Henry said. "She's in a hiking club with Ms. Mizzle. Oh, and one time I saw Ms. Mizzle wearing a yellow hat."

Dudley nodded. He was impressed.

"So do you think she's a homework robot?" Dudley asked.

Henry shrugged. "Well, I know that she's not a robot. But also my mom says that Ms. Mizzle will only assign GOOD homework."

Dudley scrunched his face. "What?! But there's NO such thing as GOOD homework!"

Henry laughed. "At least we're in the same class, so we will have the same homework!"

Dudley held out his fist, and Henry bumped it, best-friend style.

# Chapter 3

# IN
# THE BAG

Ms. Mizzle stood in front of the class. She didn't have on her yellow hat, but she *did* have on a yellow dress.

Henry wrote in his notebook, *Likes yellow*.

It was very important to get spy information right.

He also noted an empty desk in his classroom. Was a student missing? Maybe that was another mystery he could solve.

"Welcome to the first day of school!" their new teacher said in a cheery voice.

Ms. Mizzle talked about their classroom rules and introduced the class guinea pig, named Lil' Ham.

Then she held up a stack of brown paper bags.

"Does anyone know what we might do with these bags?" Ms. Mizzle asked.

Henry raised his hand. "Put stuff in them?"

"Exactly," she said. "Do you know what *kind* of stuff?"

The class guessed things like candy and bugs.

"Those are all *good* guesses," she said. "These bags are for a special project called All About Me. It works like this."

Ms. Mizzle held up a gardening glove, a book, and a tiny boot on a key chain.

"What do these things tell you about me?" she asked.

A girl with pigtails raised her hand. "You like to garden?"

"Yes!" said Ms. Mizzle.

"You like to read!" said a boy with glasses.

"And you like to HIKE!" Dudley said. He already knew this from Henry's spy list.

"Very good!" the teacher said. "Tonight I want everyone to find three things that tell us something about *you*."

Dudley raised his hand and waved it in the air. "May I put my soccer ball in the bag?"

Ms. Mizzle opened an empty bag and showed it to the class.

"Only bring things that fit in the bag," she said.

A girl in a pink top raised her hand.

"What about brand-new baby hamsters?" she said. "They are REALLY small and REALLY cute, and they would REALLY love to visit school."

Ms. Mizzle shook her head and said, "Let's leave pets at home. If you want to include them, be creative. You could draw a picture of your baby hamsters instead."

Then somebody opened the classroom door. Everyone turned to see a kid dressed in jeans, a T-shirt, and a baseball cap.

"Class, today we have a new
student at our school," said
Ms. Mizzle. "This is Mackenzie
Maplethorpe. Mackenzie just
moved to Brewster."

Henry wrote in his spy notebook, *New kid in class. Empty-desk mystery solved.*

Mackenzie pulled off her
baseball cap. Her long hair
tumbled down.

"I go by Max," she said.

Henry knew a girl named
Melanie Maplethorpe. She
was in his sister's class. Max
wasn't like Melanie as far as
Henry could tell.

"Now let's give Max a Brewster Elementary hello!" Ms. Mizzle cheered.

"Hello, Max!" the class sang.

But the new girl didn't say hello back.

# Chapter 4

# THREE THINGS

The first day of school zoomed by. Henry and Dudley counted coins in math. In science they dropped things in water to see what would float and what would sink to the bottom.

They had chicken nuggets and rainbow yogurt sticks for lunch. Then they played tag at recess.

"I love school," Henry said on the bus back home.

"Me too!" Dudley agreed. "I'm not sure that new girl liked it."

Henry nodded. "Hmm, Max didn't have a partner in math," he said.

"She ate lunch all by herself," Dudley added.

"Then, at recess, she just WATCHED everyone," Henry said as he made a note of all these things.

"Maybe the new girl wished Ms. Mizzle WAS a homework robot," Dudley said.

Henry laughed. "Maybe," he said. "We'll find out more about Max when she does her All About Me project."

The ride back went by fast, and soon the bus was at Henry's stop.

Henry waved good-bye to Dudley. Then he ran all the way home and went straight to his room.

Henry held his All About Me bag and looked around.

*Hmm,* he thought. *What three things best describe ME?*

He found his magnifying glass on the carpet.

"Well, first of all, I'm a secret spy," he said, and plopped the magnifying glass into his paper bag.

"Hey! I also love soccer." Henry grabbed his goalie gloves from a drawer in his dresser.

"Now I just need ONE more thing." Henry hunted through his toy chest.

There were stuffed animals, but nothing seemed right.

Then he turned to his bookshelf. On the very top he spied his mini remote-controlled dragon.

"That's IT!" he cried.

The toy dragon would be perfect. It had eyes that lit up. It could also roll its head, roar, and fly in a circle.

*I wonder how it got way up there,* Henry thought.

The dragon was leaning against an old book—a book that had been sitting on his shelf forever.

Henry had to find a way to get his dragon down.

# Chapter 5

# THE WEIRD OLD BOOK

Henry dragged a chair over and climbed onto it. The toy dragon was still too high.

He put one foot on the shelf and reached for the dragon again.

He could barely poke the toy with his fingertips.

And that's when his door opened.

"HENRY!" shouted his sister. "GET DOWN!"

Henry lost his balance and rolled onto the carpet like an action hero.

Things from the bookcase tumbled down. The old book landed in front of him.

"HENRY! You could have gotten hurt!" Heidi cried.

Henry rubbed his head and smiled.

"I was fine until you scared me," he said.

"I'm serious!" Heidi went on. "The bookshelf could have fallen on you!"

Henry had never thought of that.

"You better pick things up before Mom gets home," Heidi added.

Then she marched out of the room and shut the door behind her.

Henry pulled his dragon out of the mess. Luckily, nothing was broken.

Suddenly a hum sounded in the room. It was coming from the old book on the floor.

Henry touched the book, and it began to glow.

"Whoa!" whispered Henry.

## Chapter 6

# THE DRAGON SPELL

Henry opened the glowing book.

Something hard landed in his lap with a clunk. It looked like his gold soccer medal.

It had the letter *M* on it.

Henry put the medal around his neck.

Suddenly the pages of the book were turning on their own. Finally they stopped on a picture of a dragon.

"Cool!" Henry exclaimed.

Then the page turned, and a voice from nowhere read the book aloud.

# How to Get a Dragon

Have you ever wanted your very own pet dragon? A dragon that would follow you to school? Or one that would play with you? And sleep on your bed at night? If you really want a dragon, then this is the spell for you!

Ingredients:
1 picture of your favorite dragon
1 tablespoon of hot sauce
1 cup of water
2 teaspoons of baking soda

Mix the ingredients together in a bowl. Hold your medallion in one hand and place your other hand over the bowl. Chant the following spell.

# Dragon soar! And dragon dive!

# Make my dragon come ALIVE!

Note: Dragon training not included.

Magic! It was magic! Henry could not believe it.

He got the ingredients faster than a dragon could breathe fire.

Then he mixed them together,
took off the medallion, and held
it while he chanted the spell.

There was a puff of smoke,
and Henry looked around his
room.

It should have been easy to
find a real live dragon.

But Henry could not see one anywhere.

*It didn't work,* Henry thought. *Maybe I'm just a normal kid after all.*

He put the medallion back inside the book.

Henry picked up his toy dragon and said, "You're still great, even if you aren't real."

He put the toy into his bag
and started cleaning his room.

# Chapter 7

# FIRE-BREATHING FREAK-OUT!

The next morning Henry's bag felt heavier than it had the night before.

*That's odd,* Henry thought.

He peeked inside.

Magnifying glass. *Check.*

Goalie gloves. *Check*.

Dragon toy. *Check*.

Nothing had changed.

When the bus came, Henry
sat next to Dudley.

"What's in your All About
Me bag?" Henry asked.

Dudley smiled. He pulled out a stinky soccer cleat.

Next, he pulled out a pack of sour candy. Dudley loved sour candy.

And lastly, he held up his light-up yo-yo.

"Those are great!" Henry said.

"Okay, so what did YOU bring?" Dudley asked.

Henry opened his bag. The magnifying glass and the goalie gloves were there, but the dragon was *missing*.

"Oh no!" Henry cried. "My dragon is GONE!"

There was a hole in the bottom of his bag—only it wasn't just any hole. The bag had been scorched.

# Chapter 8

## SPY VS. SPY

"Don't worry. I'll help you find your toy dragon!" Dudley said. "It's not like it ran away."

The bus parked at school, and the boys waited for everyone to leave.

Dudley checked the front of the bus. Henry crawled toward the back. There, he spied his very real dragon.

He dove for it, but the dragon was fast. It flew out an open window.

Henry tried the remote control, but it didn't work.

"WOW!" Dudley cried. "I didn't know your dragon could fly like THAT!"

"Neither did I!" Henry admitted as he raced off the bus.

As Henry chased his toy, he ran smack into Max.

She dropped her All About Me bag and something rolled out. It was a magnifying glass *just* like his!

Max grabbed it and shoved
it back into her bag.

"Watch where you're going!"
she said.

"You should be careful too!"
he said, but Max was already
gone.

97

# Chapter 9

# THE WHAT-IFS

Henry couldn't decide which was worse, missing one of his All About Me items or having his real magic dragon loose in the classroom.

He squirmed in his chair.

What if the dragon lands 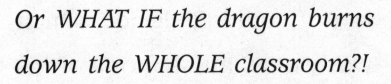 in Ms. Mizzle's hair? What if the dragon tries to eat all the kids' snacks? Or WHAT IF the dragon burns down the WHOLE classroom?!

Then Dudley nudged Henry's foot and said, "Somebody's staring at you."

Somebody *was* staring at him. But it wasn't a dragon. It was Max!

She pointed behind Henry.

He turned around.

A tiny toy dragon sat on top
of his cubby.

Henry carefully raised his hand. He did not want to scare the dragon away. He also did not want the class to see the dragon.

"Ms. Mizzle, may I please get something from my backpack?"

His teacher nodded.

Henry walked to his backpack with his best there's-no-dragon-on-top-of-my-cubby walk.

With every step Henry took, the little dragon tilted its head and flashed its red eyes playfully.

With a gulp, Henry reached for the dragon, but it flew away and Henry fell into the wall of cubbies.

Backpacks, jackets, and snacks tumbled onto the floor. The whole class laughed. At least, almost the whole class.

One student did not laugh at all: *Max*. She had seen Henry's very real dragon escape out the window.

# Chapter 10

# IT'S ONLY A TOY

The day moved slowly. All Henry could think about was finding the dragon.

Even after the cubby mess, Henry kept looking. But he didn't see anything.

Luckily, Henry made it to recess without being called on to share his All About Me bag.

He slipped on his soccer gloves and grabbed his trusty magnifying glass. It was time for a dragon hunt.

He tiptoed around the swing
set and monkey bars. Then he
spied tiny dragon paw prints.

He followed the tracks. They
led to an old oak tree.

Suddenly the dragon peeked out from the branches. It looked scared.

Henry gave a little wave and the dragon flew down to him.

He quickly cupped his hands
around the dragon when it
landed. He felt the small wings
beat against his soccer gloves.

He looked at the dragon for the first time up close.

"You are SO cute," Henry told the dragon, "but I don't

think Brewster Elementary is the best place for dragons."

The dragon's eyes flashed in agreement. It was listening to him.

Henry took a deep breath and said, "I WISH you were a TOY dragon again."

*KA-ZING!* A small glow like the one from the book surrounded the dragon. It instantly turned back into a toy.

"Wow!" Henry said aloud, just as somebody tapped him on the shoulder.

It was Max.

"You better tell me what's going on," she said.

Henry was nervous. Had Max seen anything?

"What do you mean?" he asked.

Max pointed at his dragon. "I saw that thing FLY," she said.

Henry took off his gloves and
pulled out the remote control.

"It does fly," he said. "But
it's ONLY a toy."

Then he made the dragon
fly in a circle.

"See?" he said. "By the way, I'm Henry Heckelbeck, Private Eye and Super Spy. I noticed you're a detective too." He showed her his magnifying glass.

Max reached into her All About Me bag and showed Henry *her* magnifying glass too.

"Maybe we can solve a mystery together sometime," Henry suggested.

A half smile spread across Max's face.

"Maybe," she said as the bell rang. "Because there is definitely something weird going on at this school."

Henry knew Max was right. *There WAS something weird going on here.* And Henry Heckelbeck was on the case.

# HeNRY HECKELBECK

## Never Cheats

# CONTENTS

# Chapter 1

# HEY, GOALIE!

Henry Heckelbeck pulled a round sandwich out of his lunch box. Mom had made it with a cookie cutter. Henry showed his best friend, Dudley.

"What does THIS look like?"

Dudley smiled. "It looks like a soccer ball to me!"

"RIGHT!" Henry said. "And today we have the first soccer practice after school!"

Then he held up his free hand, and Dudley smacked it.

Max Maplethorpe heard the boys as she walked by.

"What are you talking about?" she asked.

"Soccer," Dudley said.

Max sat down. "Do you play?" she asked.

Dudley's mouth fell open.

"Well, OF COURSE I play!" he said. "And for your information, I am a center back. My position tries to stop the other team from . . ."

Max held up her hand like a stop sign. "I know. I know," she said.

"You try to stop the other team from scoring a goal."

Dudley was surprised. "Do YOU play soccer?"

Max looked up from under the brim of her baseball cap. "I played goalie at my old school."

Henry smiled. "Hey, goalie!" he exclaimed. "That's what *I* play."

Max didn't say "that's cool" or anything at all. She just stared at Henry.

Henry swallowed hard. "Well, um, soccer sign-ups are at practice after school. Maybe you should join us?"

Max shrugged. "Maybe," she said.

Then she picked up her tray and walked off.

## Chapter 2

The final bell rang. Henry and Dudley grabbed their backpacks and ran to the boys' locker room.

"Do you think Max will try out?" Henry asked.

Dudley slipped a shin guard
inside his long sock.

"Who knows?" he said.
"But just in case—PLAY YOUR
BEST."

A funny feeling swept over Henry. *Dudley's right,* he thought. *What if Max is a really good goalie? What if SHE gets to play goalie and not ME?*

When Henry finished getting dressed, he joined the other kids on the field.

Principal Pennypacker stood on the sidelines in his soccer gear. The principal used to play goalie when he was in school.

Another grown-up was there. It was Mrs. Noddywonks, the drama teacher. She had on a red track suit and wore a baseball cap on top of her curly orange hair. A whistle hung around her neck.

"Welcome, soccer players!" Principal Pennypacker said. "This year, Mrs. Noddywonks is going to coach our soccer team. Now you can call her Coach!"

The kids clapped and whistled because everyone *loved* Mrs. Noddywonks.

Meanwhile, Henry saw that Max wasn't there.

His funny feeling popped like a soap bubble. *Now I'LL get to be goalie for sure!*

# Chapter 3

## UH-OH!

Coach blew her whistle. "Choose a partner and grab a ball. It's time for warm-ups!"

Henry and Dudley came together like magnets and took a black-and-white ball.

"Start with toe taps," said Coach. She placed a soccer ball in front of her. Then she tapped the  top of the ball with the toes of her cleats. First one foot, and then the other.

Each pair took turns toe-tapping a soccer ball.

"Now let's work on passes," Coach directed. "There are four steps to kicking a soccer ball.

"First you must approach the ball. Then you plant your non-kicking foot beside the ball.

Then you strike the ball with the inside of your other foot. And finally, you follow through."

Coach passed the ball to Principal Pennypacker.

Henry and Dudley passed
the ball back and forth. They
didn't miss once—until Henry
saw Max walk onto the field.

The ball whizzed past Henry.

"Dude, wake up!" Dudley cried.

Henry ran after it. That's when he overheard Coach offer to be Max's partner.

Henry turned away and
kicked the ball super hard to
Dudley. It blew past him.

While Dudley chased after
the ball, Henry spied on Max.

She had a very powerful kick. She stopped the ball really well too.

Soon the whistle blew. The players gathered around Coach.

"Okay, team! It's time for a practice game!" she said. "Who wants to play goalie?"

Henry raised his hand as high as it would go. So did Max. Then that funny feeling rushed over Henry again.

*Why does Max have to like playing goalie so much?* he wondered.

# Chapter 4

## GOALIE MOLY!

Henry and Max followed Principal Pennypacker to one of the goals for a quick and easy warm-up.

First the principal went over the rules of being a goalie.

"The lines around the goal form the penalty area," he began. "Inside this box, you can use any part of your body to stop the ball. Once you stop the ball, you have six seconds to throw or kick the ball back into play. If the ball goes out of play *behind* the goal, the goalie is awarded a goal kick."

Then Principal Pennypacker stood in goal.

"Always be in the ready position," he went on. "Stay on your toes and watch the ball move across the field. To catch the ball, hold

your hands high in a W position.

And always keep your hands on *top* of the ball."

Principal Pennypacker went to bounce the ball. He kept his arms stretched out in front of him. He caught the ball with his hands on top of the ball.

Henry watched closely. But Max acted like she knew everything already about goalkeeping. She just twirled her ponytail.

"Henry, you can go first," Principal Pennypacker said. "I'll try to score."

Henry stood in the goal.

Then the principal took a shot, and Henry blocked it with his hands.

"Very good," he said. "Now you try, Max."

Max traded places with Henry.

The principal dribbled the ball in and kicked. Max slid to one side and saved the ball with her foot.

"Well done!" the principal exclaimed.

Then Henry stepped back in the goal. He wanted to do even better this time.

The principal kicked a bouncy shot. Henry dove for it, but the ball swooshed into the back of the net.

"Nice try!" Max said as she stepped over Henry to take his place.

This time the principal kicked the shot high.

Max tapped the ball away easily with her fingertips.

Henry's jaw dropped. Max was a really good goalie. She might even be better than he was.

# Chapter 5

Coach divided the players into two teams. Henry went in goal for Team Blue. Max went in for Team Red.

Each team had five players on the field in total.

Team Blue kicked off the game. All the kids chased after the ball. They moved up and down the field like a swarm of bees.

"Spread out! Spread out!"
Coach shouted.

Dudley broke free of the swarm. He dribbled the ball and booted it toward the net. The ball shot by Max.

*Score!*

Coach blew her whistle. "Nice work!" she said. "Now everybody back in position!"

This time Team Red kicked off. They dribbled the ball into Henry's zone and took a shot.

Henry dove for it and missed.

This time Team Red cheered.

"One to one!" Coach called

out. "Tiebreaker wins!"

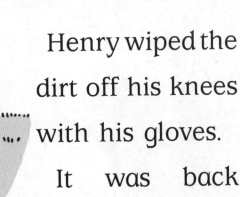

Henry wiped the dirt off his knees with his gloves.

It was back to Team Blue, but Team Red stole the ball. Then a girl with long braids kicked it out of bounds behind the goal line.

Coach blew her whistle. "Goal kick!"

Henry tried to kick the ball
to Dudley, but he slipped and
knocked the ball into his own
net. The point counted.

Max yelled, "Team Red
wins!"

Henry lay down on the field.
Dudley ran over and helped
him up.

"It was only a PRACTICE
game!" Dudley said. "So who
cares?"

Henry groaned.

"I bet a joke will help," Dudley said. "What position does a ghost play in soccer?"

Henry shrugged.

Dudley smiled. "He plays a really bad GHOUL-ie! Get it? He misses every shot because the ball goes right THROUGH him!"

Henry rolled his eyes and said, "In OUR game, *I* made all the boo-boos. . . . Get it? Ghosts? BOO! BOO!"

Dudley cracked up, and hearing his laugh made Henry feel a little better.

# Chapter 6

# SISTERLY ADVICE

Back at home Henry knocked on his sister's door. "Will you help me practice my goalie skills?"

"Why would I want to do THAT?" Heidi asked.

Henry bounced his soccer ball on the floor. "Because you can kick soccer balls at me as hard as you want."

Heidi smiled like the Grinch.
"When you put it that way,"
she said, "how can I refuse?"

In the backyard Henry told Heidi about Max.

"She's new, and she's a really good soccer goalie," Henry said. "I'm worried she is better than me."

Heidi kicked a pine cone for practice. "What's her name?" she asked.

"Her name is Max," he said. "Max Maplethorpe."

Heidi stopped and stared at Henry. "As in MELANIE MAPLETHORPE?"

"They are cousins," said Henry, and Heidi shrieked with laughter.

"If Melanie played goalie, she would need to be the star of the show!" Heidi said.

Henry folded his arms. "Max isn't like that," he said. "She's the OPPOSITE of Melanie. And she's a REALLY good goalie."

Heidi shook her head in disbelief.

"I'm not even kidding," Henry said as he set up the goal.

His sister stood over the soccer ball. "Well, YOU'RE a really good goalie too," she said.

Henry huffed. "But I still need to get better."

Heidi kicked the ball again and again. They practiced until Mom called them in for dinnertime.

As they cleaned up, Heidi nudged Henry. "Do you want some big sister advice?"

Henry nodded.

"Don't try to be BETTER than Max," she told him. "Just be the best Henry you can be. And, PS, you're a pretty good Henry Heckelbeck."

Henry bumped his sister back.

"Thanks," he said.

# Chapter 7

## CHEATER KEEPER

Henry couldn't wait to try his soccer moves at practice. Working with his sister had really helped.

"May I go first today, Coach?" Henry asked.

Coach gave him a double thumbs-up.

Henry jogged to the goal. *Be brave and throw yourself at the ball,* he told himself.

Coach kicked the ball. Henry
planted his right foot. He
pointed his knee toward the
ground. Then he collapsed on

the ball and held it tight.

"Well done!" Coach said.

Then she kicked a shot at Henry's waist. Henry caught the ball against his chest.

"Wow!" the rest of the team exclaimed.

Henry made three more solid saves. Then it was Max's turn.

Max dove for the first ball, but it bounced off her fingertips and into the goal.

"Good try," Coach said.
"Here's another."

Max stood in the ready
position with her knees bent
and hands up.

The ball came right to her, but she didn't bend over enough. The ball bounced off her chest. She kicked the dirt in anger.

During the practice game, Henry had a shutout for Team Blue, and Max let in three goals for Team Red.

Max was so mad after the game that she yelled, "Henry CHEATS!"

Max's teammates didn't like losing either.

"Yeah!" they shouted.

Coach blew her whistle sharply.

"Stop that!" she said firmly.

"We are all on the *same* team.

Let's focus on our first real game that is coming up against Frost Elementary."

Max made a sour face at Henry and whispered, "Cheater!"

Henry balled his fists. "AM NOT!" he shot back.

Then Henry and Max stormed off in different directions.

# Chapter 8

**SOCCER TRICK**

Henry ran upstairs to his room, flopped onto his bed, and screamed into his pillow.

There was a knock on his door. It was Dad. "What's wrong?" he asked.

Henry rolled over. "Max called me a CHEATER at soccer today," he said. "And I NEVER cheat!"

Dad sat on the edge of the
bed. "Of course you don't,"
he said. Then he explained
that sometimes friends say
mean things when they're
embarrassed or mad.

Henry thought about it. Max had been really upset.

Henry sighed. "I guess."

Dad smiled. "So you're good?"

Henry nodded, and Dad left the room.

*But that still doesn't give Max the right to call me a CHEATER,* Henry thought.

Then he noticed
something on the
bed beside him. It
was that weird old
book with the letter
*M* on it.

He popped out the
medallion and set it aside.

Suddenly    the
book jumped into
his   hands   and
opened all by itself.

The pages fluttered until they came to a stop on a page with a picture of a soccer ball. Underneath it was a spell.

# How to Do a Soccer Trick

Have you ever known a poor sport in soccer? Perhaps you've played a really good game and then a member of the opposite team calls you a mean name. If you think you've been treated unfairly, then this is the soccer spell for YOU!

Ingredients:
- 1 pair of outgrown pants
- 3 Red Hot candies
- 1 glass of water
- 1 toy whistle

Mix the ingredients together in a bucket. Place one hand on your medallion and place your other hand over the mix. Chant the following words.

Liar, liar, pants on fire!
Time to make another call!
From now on [person's name]
will FEAR the ball!

Note: Payback spells rarely work out the way one thinks. Kindness breaks the spell.

A smile spread across Henry's face. Maybe it was time for a little magic.

Henry gathered the ingredients and chanted the spell.

Sparkles swirled from the bucket.

Suddenly Henry couldn't wait till tomorrow's game.

# Chapter 9

# BREWSTER VERSUS FROST

The Frost Elementary team arrived right after school. Everyone warmed up on the field.

"Max, you'll start in goal," Coach said.

Henry folded his arms. *Why does MAX get to start?* he wondered.

Then Henry remembered the spell. If it worked, then he would be goalie in no time.

Brewster had the ball first. They kept it in the offensive zone far away from Max. Dudley cross-kicked the ball in front of the net.

With a slide, the Frost goalie saved the shot! Then she kicked the ball. It whizzed by all the players and headed right to Max.

Max waited eagerly, but then the spell kicked in. *Zing!* When the ball reached her, Max squealed and jumped away. The ball slowly rolled into the goal. Frost had scored.

Henry covered his mouth to hide a laugh. The game restarted, and Frost stole the ball. A boy with spiky hair kicked it toward the goal.

Max didn't try to catch the ball. She *dodged* it! The ball smacked into the back of the net. Frost scored again!

The Brewster players were upset. Everyone except Henry.

Finally the whistle blew for halftime. Poor Max ran off the field and hid.

*Ha! Now it's my turn!* Henry thought. *Time to save the day!*

# Chapter 10

# A BAD SPELL

"Your turn in goal, Henry," Coach said. Henry hopped up from the bench. Then he saw Max. She was sitting all by herself. Tears streamed down her cheeks.

*Wow, she's REALLY sad,* Henry realized. *And it's all MY fault.*

Then he remembered his sister's advice: *Just be the BEST Henry you can be.*

Henry hung his head. He had not been a very good Henry at all.

He walked over to Max. She rubbed her eyes and looked up at Henry.

"What are you going to do?"
she asked. "Make fun of me?"
Henry    shook    his    head.

"Actually, I just want you to know that you're an awesome goalie," he said. "Everybody has a BAD SPELL once in a while."

Then Henry called the team over. "Everyone, I have something to say. Max is a really good goalie who had

some bad luck. But we NEED her right now. Max is the one who should be in goal."

Coach smiled and asked if Max still wanted to play.

"You can do it," Henry told her. "I KNOW you can."

"I'll do it," said Max.

The Brewster players all clapped for their goalie.

Henry sat back down on the bench. Principal Pennypacker slid beside him.

"Seems you have a *magical* gift for coaching," he said.

Before Henry could answer, a Frost player kicked the ball on goal. Max dove for it and grabbed the ball out of the air. It was a spectacular save! The spell had been broken!

The crowd cheered, but Henry cheered the loudest. It felt good to be the best Henry he could be.

# HeNRY HECKELBECK

## and the Haunted Hideout

# CONTENTS

# Chapter 1

# BACKYARD
# SPIES

Dudley Day whispered, "I spy an anthill!"

Henry Heckelbeck joined his best friend to watch the ants. They both wondered if the ants had secret tunnels inside.

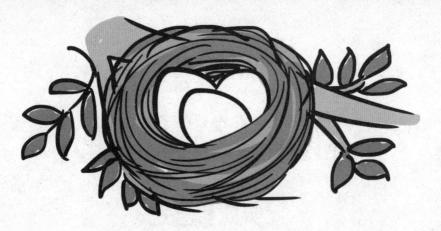

"I spy a bird's nest!" cried Henry, pointing his binoculars at the treetops. "Wouldn't a nest make a cool hangout?"

Dudley stood up and said, "Yeah. So would an anthill."

Then Henry spotted a red-orange cat in the garden.

"I spy something FURRY," he whispered. The cat belonged to the next-door neighbors. Henry had nicknamed him Kevin.

Dudley tiptoed to Henry's side. "Let's follow it!" he said.

The boys tracked Kevin along
the stone wall and down into
Henry's dad's vegetable patch.
Kevin stopped and chewed on
some spinach.

"Ew!" the boys cried.

Then Kevin trotted toward the house and leaped onto a windowsill.

The boys crouched under the window. They slowly stood up to spy on the cat, but Kevin bounded away.

Now the only things in the window were Henry and Dudley.

Henry could see his sister, Heidi. She was inside the house with her friends Bruce Bickerson and Lucy Lancaster. Then Heidi saw Henry.

"HEY!" she shouted at her brother. "Quit SPYING on us!"

Henry and Dudley ran away before they got blamed for anything else Kevin did.

# Chapter 2

## ON A MISSION

"What WE need is a space of our own!" Henry declared.

Dudley nodded. "Someplace where nobody can bug us!"

The boys had a new mission: Secret Hideout Search.

First they tried behind the
bushes in Henry's backyard.

"Not roomy enough," Henry
said.

Next they checked behind
the fence, but a grapevine was
in the way.

"Look over here," said
Dudley. He led Henry under
the branches of
a pine tree.

Then they
heard Heidi
yelling from
inside the
house.

"I can STILL see you!" she shouted.

"Merg," said Henry. "Let's get out of here."

The boys got permission to go to Charmed Court Park down the street. They raced all the way there.

"Hey, let's look inside that hedge!" Dudley suggested.

The boys slid sideways into the middle of the hedge. It was nice and roomy inside—a perfect place for a hideout, except for one thing. They had crossed into squirrel territory.

*"Kuk! Kuk! Kuk!"* an angry squirrel scolded, and it charged at them.

*"AAAAAAAH!"* squealed the boys as they scrambled out of the hedge.

"Forget THAT!" Henry said.

Dudley brushed off his shirt and asked, "Now what do we do?"

Henry thought for a moment. "Now we race to the top of the climbing wall at the playground!" he said. "Ready? GO!"

The boys dashed to the wall and climbed up like daddy longlegs.

"WE TIED!" Henry shouted when they reached the top at the same time. Then they peered into the opening where the three walls connected.

"Look down there!" Dudley said, pointing to the space below. "That would make a GREAT hideout!"

The boys hopped down into the space.

"Wow, this place is like an anthill, only for KIDS!" Dudley exclaimed.

Henry leaned his head against the wall. "And best of all, Heidi will NEVER find us in here!"

## Chapter 3

# WHO GOES THERE?

The next day the boys spied somebody reading a book in their secret No-Heidi Hideout.

"WHO GOES THERE?" Henry shouted. "And you better not be my sister!"

It was Max Maplethorpe, the new girl in Henry and Dudley's class.

"It's ME," said Max.

Both of the boys wrinkled their noses.

"You DARE to invade our secret hideout?" Dudley asked.

Max frowned and said, "This place is no secret."

The boys sighed heavily and lowered themselves into the den.

"Secret hideouts are sure hard to come by," Henry complained.

"You're not kidding," said Max as she pointed to the opening at the top. The boys looked  up and saw lots of little kids peering down at them.

"Oh no!" cried Henry. "MORE
invaders! Now we have to find
another hideout!"

# Chapter 4

# THE MAGIC SEED

By dinnertime the boys hadn't found anything.

Henry went home and flopped onto his bed. He felt something weird under his pillow. It was that old book!

He stared at the cover, and it opened up *by itself*! Then the medallion inside floated right out of the book!

The chain circled around Henry's head and gently came to rest around his neck. Pages in the book fluttered and stopped on a spell that Henry read over.

# How to Plant a Secret Hideout

Have you ever wanted a private space to hide out with your friends? Perhaps you'd like to get away from an annoying sibling or snoopy kids in general? Well, if you're in need of a secret hideout, then this spell is for you!

Ingredients:

1 secret wish, written down
2 left-footed socks
1 pair of sunglasses
1 mirror

Mix the ingredients together in a bowl. Then hold your hand palm-side up to receive a magic seed. Chant the following spell:

A nest! A lair! A cubbyhole!
A place for friends to go.
Grant me now a hidey-hole!
A seed that I can sow!

Note: Plant the seed wherever you want your hideout. The hideout will only be visible to you and your friends.

Henry quickly wrote down
his wish:

one
AWESOME
hideout

Then he grabbed two socks
from his dresser, a pair of
sunglasses from his beach bag,
and a toy mirror from Heidi's
pretend makeup kit.

Henry mixed the ingredients together and chanted the spell. A burst of sparkles shimmered over the bowl, and then a magic seed appeared in his hand.

# Chapter 5

# WHOOPS!

Henry clutched the seed in his fist. *Now I need to find the PERFECT secret hideout spot!*

He ran to the playroom. Heidi twirled on the swing that hung from the ceiling.

*Not in here!* he thought.

Henry circled through the dining room, the kitchen, and the den. *Mom would never allow a hideout in any of THESE rooms,* he thought.

Henry kept going until he found Heidi again! She was lying on the sofa.

"Not YOU again!"
she sneered.

Henry stuck out
his tongue and
disappeared into
the backyard. *Maybe I'll plant
the hideout somewhere sneaky,*
he thought.

Then Kevin the cat trotted
over. Henry knelt down to say
hello, but Kevin jumped into
Henry's lap.

Henry lost his balance and dropped the magic seed—right in the middle of the yard.

"Oh no!" Henry cried as Kevin scampered away. "Not HERE!"

But it was too late. The seed
instantly grew into a giant
round bush.

"Now EVERYONE will know
where my secret hideout is!"
Henry grumbled.

Then Henry remembered something: The hideout would only be visible to him and his friends.

Henry quickly found the opening and climbed inside.

"WHOA!" he cried. "This place is COOL-O NOOL-O!"

The magic hideout had lots of space and a thick web of branches all around. There was even enough sunlight to play games or do homework. It was perfect!

Then Henry heard his mother calling him for dinner. He left the hideout and ran all the way to the house.

Before he opened the back door, he turned around to make *sure* the secret hideout was really there.

And sure enough, it *really* was.

# Chapter 6

# WHAT WAS THAT?

The next day Henry showed Dudley the secret hideout.

"How did we miss this?!" Dudley exclaimed. "Has this bush been here all along?"

Henry thought fast.

"Uh, no," he said. "We JUST got this bush!"

Dudley bought it. "Well, it's totally cool!"

The boys climbed in and set up their stuff.

"Guess what I brought?" Dudley said as he pulled opened his backpack.

Henry rubbed his hands together and guessed, "Hmm, is it something to eat?"

Dudley nodded. "Bananas! Brownies! And chips!"

One by one he laid out the snacks. Dudley took a brownie, and Henry chose a banana.

While they were munching, they heard a strange sound in the branches above them.

"What in the world is that noise?" whispered Dudley.

Henry shook his head. "I don't know," he said, his heart beating faster.

The boys sat very still and listened. Something rustled inside the branches.

The leaves shook. Then, all at once, the entire bush began to shake.

The boys squealed. Then they pushed and shoved each other out of the hideout. They sat on the ground and caught their breath.

"Maybe Heidi's pranking us," said Henry.

The boys searched the entire backyard. They didn't see Heidi anywhere.

When the spooky feelings
had worn off, the boys crawled
back into the hideout.

"Seems normal now," Henry
said.

Dudley nodded and picked
up his joke book to read.

Henry decided to finish his banana. He pulled back the rest of the peel, but the banana was all gone.

"That's weird," Henry said. "I thought I had a little banana left."

Dudley looked up from his joke book. "That IS weird. Because you know what ghosts love to eat?"

Henry shrugged.

Dudley smiled and yelled, "BOO-nanas!"

# Chapter 7

# NOT AGAIN!

For a week the hideout stayed as normal as a magic hideout could be. Henry was sitting inside with his spy notebook, when a hand pulled back the branches.

It was Dudley, but he wasn't alone. Max was with him.

"Uh, hi, Henry," Dudley mumbled. "I kinda, sorta ran into Max and kinda, sorta told her about your hideout, and she kinda, sorta wanted to see it."

Max looked over Dudley's shoulder. "And the little kids at the rock-climbing wall wouldn't leave me alone. I just want a quiet place to hang out."

Henry knew what *that* felt like.

"Okay, sure. Come in," he said.

"This place is spectacular!" Max said as she entered. "It's like a dome made of branches!"

Henry smiled. He was very proud of his magical hideout.

The three friends settled in. Max read her book, and Henry and Dudley went over their spy notes from school.

"Did you know Principal

Pennypacker had a cream-cheese-and-olive sandwich for lunch today?" Henry asked.

Dudley scrunched his nose. "That's gross."

Henry nodded. "And did you know the water fountain overflowed today?" he asked. "I reported it to Mr. Fortini."

"What caused it?" Dudley asked.

"Bubble gum."

Dudley made a note of it.

Suddenly the rustling began again. Max set down her book. The three friends froze and stared into the branches.

Then—*SHOOP!*—Max's book slid across the floor by itself. The kids squished themselves into the corner.

"Guys, is this a prank?" Max whispered. "Because it isn't funny!"

Henry and Dudley stared at Max with huge owl eyes.

"We're not doing anything," Henry whispered.

Then Dudley pointed at Max's head. "Max, does your baseball cap normally float above your head?"

Max looked up at her floating hat and screamed.

The kids darted out of the hideout as fast as possible and tumbled onto the lawn, gasping for breath.

Max was the first to speak. "Guys!" she cried. "Your hideout is TOTALLY HAUNTED!"

# Chapter 8

## GHOST ZAPPER

Max dusted herself off and put her hat back on.

"Today is your lucky day to have a haunted hideout," she told the boys, "because I am an expert ghost zapper!"

Henry and Dudley looked at each other.

"A WHAT?" they asked.

Max helped them up. "I know how to remove ghosts. We had some in our old garage that made the same exact noises as your ghost. Do you want to know why?"

Henry and Dudley nodded.

"YOU are in the ghost's personal space," she told them. "Would you like help getting rid of the ghost?"

The boys nodded again.

"Okay, let's go!" Max cried as she climbed back into the hideout. "All you have to do is follow my directions."

The boys carefully went in after her.

Max called out to the ghost.
"Oh, Ghost! Tell us your
demands!"

Immediately, the bush
shook. Henry
and Dudley
grabbed hold
of each other.

"Now that we have the ghost's attention, we can begin," explained Max. "First you have to clap loudly."

The boys let go of each other and began to clap as loudly as they could.

Max nodded. "Now stomp your feet at the same time and move in a circle!"

The boys did as Max said.
"Very good!" she said. "Now
cluck like a chicken."

The boys clapped, stomped, and clucked in a circle.

"Cluck even LOUDER!" Max demanded.

The boys clucked louder.

"Wow, that's REALLY good!" Max said. "Now you have to ACT like a ghost!"

The boys held their arms out and began to moan and groan.

Max looked up at the branches. "It's WORKING!"

The boys kept at it until Max held up her hand like a stop sign.

"YOU DID IT! The ghost is GONE!"

Both of the boys stopped and listened. They didn't hear any rustling.

But they did hear another sound. It was the sound of Max laughing her head off.

# Chapter 9

# THE CAT AND THE HAT

"What's so funny?" Henry asked.

"YOU ARE!" Max roared.

Henry and Dudley didn't understand.

"Don't you get it?" said Max.

"There never WAS a ghost!"

Both boys folded their arms.

"You mean we acted like chickens for no reason?" Dudley asked.

Max fell to the ground laughing. "YUP! And you should have seen yourselves!"

The boys watched in disbelief.

"Then who made all those creepy rustling sounds?" asked Henry.

"I'll show you!" said Max.

Then she clicked her tongue
and rubbed two fingers
together.

Soon a furry face poked through the branches.

It was *Kevin*!

"Here's your 'ghost'!" Max declared. "I saw him when I got here. I thought you knew he was hiding. When you jumped at the rustling sounds, I decided to play a prank on you!"

Henry and Dudley both
screamed about being so silly.

"Wow, you totally GOT US!"
said Henry.

Then they all burst out laughing.

"But how did your book slide across the floor?" Dudley asked.

"The cat batted it away, and it went flying!" said Max. "The same with my cap. The cat lifted it off my head with its claws."

Henry and Dudley shook their heads. It had been the perfect prank. And the boys *loved* pranks—even when the prank was on them.

Dudley scooped up Kevin into his arms. "You are a little troublemaker!" he said, rubbing his cheek on Kevin's fur.

Then Dudley let out a giant sneeze. Then another, and another, and another!

"Uh-oh. Are you allergic to cats?" asked Max.

Dudley sniffled and said, "Maybe I am!"

They put Kevin outside—
even though Henry knew
perfectly well Kevin would
come right back in.

"Well, it looks like we need
to find another new hideout,"
Henry announced.

# Chapter 10

# UP A TREE

This time Henry and Dudley wanted a tree house. There was a perfect tree in Dudley's backyard. Henry's dad agreed to help them build it on one condition: The kids had to help.

Dad created the plans on his computer. Then they picked out wood at the lumberyard. Dad did most of the carpentry. Henry helped build the ladder.

Dudley and Max collected
things to furnish the tree
house. Max brought four
foam chairs from her house.

Dudley brought a rug. And Henry found a round table in the basement.

Dad installed three windows in the hideout. He placed pegs on the wall to hang jackets and spy gear. He also made a special trapdoor entrance to keep out critters.

"There's no way Kevin can
get in now!" Dudley said.

Henry shared a look with Max. They both knew cats can climb almost anywhere, but they didn't share that with Dudley.

When the tree house was done, the friends hung a sign on the outside that read:

Then they sat on the comfy foam chairs and had their first official secret hideout meeting.

As they talked, a pebble ticked off the side of the tree house.

Henry peeked out one of the windows.

It was Heidi and her friends Lucy and Bruce.

"Hey there, my favorite little brother," Heidi said sweetly. "Can we come over for a visit? Please?"

Henry smirked because he was Heidi's *only* little brother. Still, he really wanted to show off their new hideout.

"Sure," he said. "I have to warn you, though. . . . They say this place is haunted."

*Haunted by a cat named Kevin,* thought Henry. *But Heidi and her friends don't need to know that. Mwoo-hoo-haa-haa-haa*

# HENRY HECKELBECK

## Spells Trouble

# CONTENTS

# Chapter 1

## SPELL CHECK

It was a quiet day at Brewster Elementary. Henry Heckelbeck opened his spy notebook and picked up a pen.

"Got any NEW secret INFO?" he asked Dudley Day.

Dudley smiled. "Yup. See that kid on the kickball field? The one at home plate?"

Henry nodded.

"Well, that kid USUALLY kicks with his RIGHT foot," Dudley explained. "But watch closely."

Henry watched the boy kick the ball. "Whoa, he just kicked with his LEFT! Good one, Dudster."

Henry made a note of it. Then he shared something he had spied. "Did you see that third grader who got a buzz cut? Now you can see where his tan line stops!"

Dudley laughed. "He has a racing stripe on his neck!"

Henry jotted down *racing stripe*.

"And guess what else?" Henry said. "Maddie Martinez forgot her new glasses today. She keeps pulling off her old pink frames and blinking a lot."

Dudley nodded. "Well, I hope she didn't lose her new frames. They have little stars INSIDE the plastic."

Henry jotted this down too.

"I have one more spy note," Dudley went on. "Your sister's teacher only took one bite of her sandwich today."

Henry scrunched his nose.
"Ew. Maybe it had MOLDY
cheese!"

That made Dudley giggle.
Then somebody *behind* them
giggled too.

It was Max Maplethorpe.
She had been watching over
their shoulders.

"What in the world are you
doing?" Henry cried.

Max smirked. "Reading your SPY NOTES!"

Henry slapped his notebook shut. "It's a flip-flop, Dudley! The spies have been SPIED on!"

Max took a step back.

"Hey! Take it easy!" she said. "Remember, I'm a fellow spy! And for your information, you misspelled three words in your book."

"Where?" Henry asked.

"'Glasses' has three s's," Max said. "And 'kickball' is ONE word—not TWO. And there's no 'WITCH' in 'sandwich.'"

Henry checked his spelling and said, "Merg! You're right!"

Max smiled and arched the bill of her baseball cap.

"Looks like you guys better brush up on your spelling," she added. "Because it's almost time for the Brewster Spelling Bee . . . and I plan to W-I-N."

# Chapter 2

# WORKER BEES

"Hocus-pocus! Time to focus!" called the teacher, Ms. Mizzle. The class became quiet.

"I have some exciting news!" she said. "This year we will join the Brewster Spelling Bee."

Henry slumped in his chair.
*Ugh, Max was right again!*

Henry did *not* like the idea of spelling words in front of other people. He looked to Dudley for help, but Dudley just shrugged.

A girl named Stella Shah raised her hand and asked, "How does a spelling bee work? And does it sting?"

"Excellent questions, Stella," said Ms. Mizzle. "First, no, a spelling bee doesn't sting. It's not a bee at all! It's a contest where students in different classes compete by spelling words!"

Stella let out a big *Phew!*

Then Ms. Mizzle continued. "Okay a spelling bee has three jobs. The word giver, each speller, and the judge. The word giver says the word to be spelled. The speller *spells* the word. And the judge decides if the word was spelled correctly. Any questions?"

Dudley raised his hand. "How much time do you get to spell a word?"

Ms. Mizzle held up two fingers. "Two minutes."

Max's hand shot up next. "Do you get a prize if you win?"

Ms. Mizzle nodded. "Yes, Max, a prize will be given for the winner in each grade."

Dudley's hand shot up again. "Where is the spelling bee going to *bee* held?"

Ms. Mizzle laughed and checked her notes.

"The spelling bee will be held on the Brewster stage. Each grade will take turns during the day. Our class will go last. Family and friends are all invited too! Isn't this *exciting*?" she said.

Then the class began to all talk at once. Henry just picked at the corner of his desk.

He did not think a spelling bee sounded exciting. It sounded *terrifying*.

# Chapter 3

## BEE QUIET!

Henry planted his broccoli deep into the soft part of his baked potato at dinner. Then he sprinkled shredded cheddar cheese on top of his broccoli forest.

"How was school?" asked Dad.

"Pretty good," he said. He wasn't about to mention the spelling bee.

But then his sister, Heidi, made it a news flash.

"School was BEEautiful! It's time for the Brewster Spelling Bee!" she said.

"How fun," said Mom.

"And you know what ELSE?" Heidi asked.

Mom and Dad shook their heads.

"Family and friends can come to cheer for everyone! And MORE great news!" Heidi went on. "This year *I* plan to compete!"

Mom and Dad noticed that Henry wasn't as excited as his sister.

"You're being quiet, Henry,"
Mom said. "What about you?"
"What ABOUT me?" he said,
not looking up from his plate.

Mom tried again. "Are you going to take part in the spelling bee too?"

Henry pushed his plate away. "Do I have a choice?"

Dad reached over and patted Henry on the back. "I happen to know that you are a *great* speller! You can even wear my lucky *bumblebee* bow tie! Would you do it then?"

Henry crossed his arms.
"Not if I don't have to."

Heidi frowned at her brother.
Then she turned back to Mom
and Dad.

"Well, I'VE already started to practice MY spelling," she said. "Give me a word—ANY WORD—and I'll spell it for you!"

Dad stroked his chin. "How about the word 'crowd'? As in: We will be in the *crowd* cheering for you both."

Heidi took the saltshaker and held it like a microphone.

"Crowd," she repeated. "C-R-
O-W-D. That spells 'crowd.'"

Henry knew he was doomed.
There was no escape. He had
to do the spelling bee whether
he liked it or N-O-T.

# Chapter 4

# BEE-WARE!

Henry crawled into bed that night and pulled the covers over his head.

All he could think about was the spelling bee.

Soon he began to dream.

Suddenly Henry stood on a center stage—all alone. The room was dark, but Henry could see the crowd in their seats.

A spotlight switched on, and the light beamed on Henry. He covered his eyes with his arm.

Then he heard a noise.

*BUZZZZZZZZ*.

The spotlight moved away

from Henry and landed on a

*giant bee.*

The bee's face looked a little like Principal Pennypacker's— which was really weird. Plus, he had the body of a bumblebee, and he was flying!

Henry swallowed hard. "Who are YOU?" he asked.

The bee laughed loudly. "Why, I am the Spelling Bee!

I'll be your host for today's Buzzy Brewster Spelling Bee!"

The giant bee turned to face the crowd as they clapped and cheered.

"Our contestant is Henry Heckelbeck from Ms. Mizzle's class," the Spelling Bee said as he turned toward Henry. "Your word is 'mudollop.'"

The spotlight shifted back to Henry. He shoved his hands deep into the pockets of his pants.

"Is that even a REAL word?" Henry asked. His voice boomed from the speakers.

The Spelling Bee smiled and waited for Henry to spell the word.

"Can you use the word in a sentence?" Henry asked.

The bee nodded.

"Yes, you *can* use 'mudollop' in a sentence," he replied. "You see? I *just* did!"

Henry felt his face grow warm. "But can you use the  word in a sentence that makes SENSE?"

The smile left the Spelling Bee's face. He stuck out his lower lip.

"Oh dear, Henry Heckelbeck from Ms. Mizzle's class," he said. "I can see that you're not ready for the spelling bee."

The whole audience gasped. "Look at Henry Heckelbeck," they chanted. "He's not ready. He's NOT READY!"

Then the Spelling Bee flew above center stage. The crowd stopped chanting.

"What's the matter with Henry?" the bee asked the crowd. "Has the cat got his tongue?" Then the crowd began to laugh and point.

Henry looked to see where they were pointing. He saw a *giant cat* creeping across the stage. Henry tried to run away. But his feet wouldn't move! It was like they were glued to the floor.

"HELP! Somebody, HELP!" he cried. "The cat's trying to get my TONGUE!"

Suddenly Henry sat upright in bed. His alarm clock was buzzing—just like a *bee*. Henry slapped the off button.

*It was only a bad dream!* he thought. Henry wiped his brow and realized something. The dream was fake, but the spelling bee at school was still very, very real.

And he wasn't ready.

# Chapter 5

# BUSY BEES

Instead of his spy notebook, Henry brought a dictionary to recess.

"Come on!" he said to Dudley. "Let's practice for the spelling bee."

Dudley followed Henry to the side of the school building. Nobody would bother them there. The boys sat down and leaned against the wall. Henry opened the dictionary to the letter *M*.

"Have you ever heard of the word 'mudollop'?" Henry asked.

Dudley shook his head. "Nope. Definitely not."

Henry ran his fingers down the pages.

"Well, last night I dreamed about the spelling bee. I got the word 'mudollop,' and I want to see if it exists." Henry tried two different spellings. But neither one was in the dictionary. "The word seemed so REAL in my dream!"

Dudley laughed. "You are so W-E-I-R-D," he said, spelling the word out.

Somebody else laughed too. The boys looked up. It was Max, of course.

"Whatcha doing, guys?" she asked.

Dudley lifted the dictionary. "We're practicing our S-P-E-L-L-I-N-G," he said. "And I just made up a new R-U-L-E. From now on, we have to spell one W-O-R-D in every sentence we say."

Max sat down in front of the boys and wrapped her arms around her knees.

"Okay," she said. "You want some H-E-L-P?"

Before anyone could answer, Max held up her hand. "Wait! I actually have some S-P-Y info to share."

Henry and Dudley leaned in closer.

She whispered, "Well, it's about Principal Pennypacker. He's wearing a Band-Aid on his F-I-N-G-E-R. But it's not just ANY Band-Aid. It's a . . . G-L-I-T-T-E-R Band-Aid."

The boys' mouths dropped
open.

"Whoa, why would the principal wear a G-L-I-T-T-E-R Band-Aid?" Dudley asked.

Max shrugged. "Who knows?" she said. "But it makes him look M-A-G-I-C."

Dudley laughed and said, "A MAGIC principal? But he doesn't even have a long white beard or a pointy H-A-T!"

Then Max pinched her lips together. "I didn't say he WAS M-A-G-I-C. I said he LOOKED M-A-G-I-C."

Henry shook his head at Dudley, like *duh*. All this talk about magic was making him a little nervous. So he changed the subject.

"Are you going to H-E-L-P us or not?" he asked Max.

Max smiled as she took the dictionary from Henry.

"Y-E-S!" she said.

# Chapter 6

# RELAX, BEE HAPPY!

At home, Henry sat on his bedroom floor with the family dictionary. He had messy hair and dark circles under his eyes. He looked like he hadn't slept for days and days.

Heidi stood in the doorway.

"You look like a wreck," she said.

"Thanks," Henry answered without looking up from the dictionary.

Then Heidi whipped out a piece of paper from behind her back.

"Guess what I have?" she said, lifting her eyebrows. "Last year's spelling bee words for your grade. I can test you if you want."

Henry shut the dictionary.

"Really?" he asked. "That would be great!"

Heidi sat down on the floor opposite Henry. Then she read each word out loud—"cake," "bike," "crab," "kick," and "soccer."

Henry spelled every word right—even "soccer."

"See?" his sister said, folding the word list into a small square. "You have nothing to worry about."

Henry bit his lip. "It's not the SPELLING I'm worried about."

Heidi folded her arms. She knew her brother wasn't telling her everything. "Then what is it?"

"You have to promise not to laugh," Henry said.

Heidi promised. She even crossed her heart, and that was enough for Henry.

Suddenly all his fears tumbled out.

"I'm kind of scared of being onstage," he said. "What if I trip? Or what if I burp in the middle of a word? What if everyone laughs at me?"

Henry's heart was racing fast. "Or WHAT IF . . . a GIANT CAT tries to get my tongue?!"

Finally Heidi held up her hand to stop her brother.

"Whoa!" she cried. "You've got it ALL wrong! Spelling bees are FUN. They're way easier than blocking a penalty kick in soccer. And you do that ALL the time!"

Henry sat up. "Penalty kicks?
I LOVE to block penalty kicks!"
Heidi smiled. "Then the
spelling bee will be a snap!"

"What if I get everything wrong?" asked Henry.

"You know what happens if you misspell a word?" Heidi said. "You get to sit and watch the rest of the class!"

*That doesn't sound too bad,* Henry thought.

But he knew one thing for sure: He definitely didn't want a giant cat to get his tongue.

# Chapter 7

## BEE CALM

Henry stared at the glow-in-the-dark stars on his ceiling. He did not want to fall asleep. What if he had another bad dream? He rolled over and plumped his pillow.

Then something caught his attention.

A ball of light started to glow on his bookshelf. Henry sat forward as the glow began to float through the air . . . toward him. It was that weird old book again!

A medallion slid out of the book. The chain circled Henry's head and came to rest around his neck. Then the book landed gently in his lap and opened to a spell.

# A Honey of a Spell~ing Bee

Are you the kind of wizard who thinks spelling bees are scary? Perhaps you don't like to spell words in front of other people. Or maybe you're too worried about being onstage. If you think the cat is trying to get your tongue, then this is the spell for you!

Ingredients:
1 tablespoon of honey
2 flakes of lavender soap
1 pocket-size dictionary
3 deep breaths

Mix the ingredients together in a bowl and take three deep breaths. Hold your medallion in one hand and hold your other hand over the mix. Chant the following spell.

To have a happy spelling bee,
Honey, be calm. That's the key!
Now say it out loud: "I am free!
And stage fright is no part of me!"

Note: This spell has side effects. It may attract buzzy buddies and cause old-fashioned talk. To break the spell, do something unselfish.

Henry couldn't believe his luck. This was the *perfect* spell for him—and it wasn't even cheating! The magic would only work to keep him calm.

Henry tiptoed out of bed and collected all the ingredients.

He stirred the mix, took three deep breaths, and cast the spell.

*Whoosh!* A feeling of peace washed over Henry, and he fell fast asleep.

# Chapter 8

## BEE READY

The next morning, Mom handed Henry a mixed-berry smoothie for breakfast.

"A thousand thank-yous, Mother," Henry said. "What a fine way to start the day!"

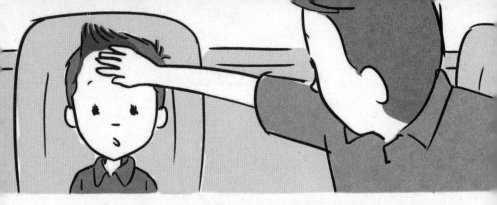

Dad reached over and put his hand on Henry's forehead. "Are you feeling all right?"

Henry blushed. *The spell wasn't kidding about side effects,* he thought. Then he tried to talk normally.

"I've never been better, Father!" Henry said in NOT a normal way. "Do you and Mother still plan to attend the spelling bee today?"

Dad looked at Heidi and raised his eyebrows. Heidi shrugged and looked at Mom. Mom shook her head and looked back at Dad. So Dad played along.

"Yes, Son," he said. "Mother and I shall both attend the spelling bee this afternoon!"

*Phew! Dad thinks I'm joking!* Henry thought.

"You are so amusing, dear Father!" responded Henry. "I shall see you later!"

On the way to the bus, Heidi said, "Please knock off the old-timey talk, Henry. It's REALLY weird."

Henry nodded and kept his mouth shut. He didn't want his friends to hear him either. What would they think?

He decided to keep quiet until *after* the spelling bee.

Henry was silent all day. He did his math in the math corner.

He wrote his soccer paragraph alone in the library.

He ate lunch at his desk and studied his spelling words. Nobody even noticed because the whole class was studying for the spelling bee.

Finally Ms. Mizzle chimed
her triangle. "Time to line up
for the spelling bee!"

Everyone pushed back their chairs and raced to the door. Then the class filed into the auditorium and climbed the stairs onto the stage. The crowd was already seated. Henry spotted his parents and waved.

*Wow,* he thought. *I don't feel one bit afraid!*

The spell had worked.

# Chapter 9

# BEE CAREFUL!

The class sat side by side in grown-up chairs so big that no one's feet reached the floor.

Henry sat on his hands and swung his legs back and forth. He felt great.

Soon Principal Pennypacker welcomed everyone, and the spelling bee began. He called Henry's name first. Henry hopped from his seat and walked to the microphone.

"Henry, your word is 'carry,'" said the principal. "As in: Please help me *carry* these heavy books. Carry."

Henry leaned toward the microphone.

"Carry," he repeated. "C-A-R-R-Y. Carry."

Principal Pennypacker nodded.

"Very good, Henry!"

The audience clapped.

"Woo!" shouted Dad.

Then Henry swore he could hear a bumblebee buzzing in the room. *That's weird,* he thought.

He watched Dudley and Max spell the words "soggy" and "wink" correctly. After they went, Maddie Martinez spelled "coat" wrong.

"I'm sorry," said the principal. "That spelling is incorrect."

Henry watched Maddie leave
the stage. She was smiling and
happy and didn't seem upset
at all. Plus, the audience still
clapped for her! Maybe this
would be easier than he had
originally thought.

When they reached the final round, it was Henry against Max!

Max went first. She spelled the word "buzz": B-U-Z-Z.

And "buzz" was the right word! As soon as she finished, Henry heard a swarm of bees.

Then Henry stepped forward and saw them! There were bees buzzing above the audience.

The crowd noticed them too. People started to get up and leave!

 That was when Henry  remembered the note about side effects from the spell.

OH NO! he thought. *I've*  *been talking, and honey* words *can bring buzzy*  *buddies. . . . That means I'm* *attracting bees whenever I talk!*

# Chapter 10

## BEE BRAVE

Henry could not remember how to break the spell. Was there a special word? Did he need to eat honey? What was it?!

Then it came to him. Being unselfish was the key.

Henry stood in front of the microphone and knew exactly what to do.

"Okay, Henry, your next word is 'magic,'" the principal said. "As in: Sometimes *magic* can spell trouble. Magic."

Henry gulped.

*Does Principal Pennypacker KNOW something? But how? There's NO way.* He took a deep breath.

"Magic . . . ," he repeated. "M-A-J-I-K. Magic."

Henry's body twitched and the buzzing hum of the bees disappeared. The spell had been broken.

Henry heard his sister and his parents gasp. Not because they noticed the spell. They just couldn't believe Henry had misspelled "magic"!

Then Max saw her chance and raced to the microphone. "MAGIC," she said loudly. "M-A-G-I-C. Magic."

The principal turned to the crowd and announced, "We have a WINNER!"

The crowd erupted with claps and cheers as Principal Pennypacker placed a medal around Max's neck.

Henry congratulated Max. "Way to go!" he said.

But Max wrinkled her nose at Henry. "Did you spell that last word wrong to help me win?"

"Why would I do that?" Henry said.

"I don't know, but I'm keeping an eye on you, Henry Heckelbeck!" Max said as she ran to her family.

Then somebody slapped Henry on the back. He turned around and saw his sister and parents.

"Great job!" Heidi cried. "I didn't even make it out of round two this year!"

"We're proud of you, Henry!" Dad said. "May we take you out to dinner tonight? Your choice."

"YES!" Henry cried. "Can we have P-I-Z-Z-A? Because I'm STARVING."

Dad winked. "In that case, we'd better *bee* going!"

"O-K!" Henry said.

And the whole family laughed because Henry had the last *word*.

Henry Heckelbeck and his best friend, Dudley Day, raced into the backyard.

Both boys stared at the tops of the trees. They watched the leaves flutter in the wind.

An excerpt from *Henry Heckelbeck and the Race Car Derby*

"This is a PERFECT kite day," Henry declared.

"Finally!" agreed Dudley. The boys had been waiting for a windy day for weeks.

They grabbed their kites, invited Henry's dad, and then went to the park.

Henry had a green-purple-and-blue kite. Dudley had a big rainbow-colored kite that was shaped like a diamond.

An excerpt from *Henry Heckelbeck and the Race Car Derby*

At the park, the boys passed a kickball game, picnickers, and a dad playing catch with his daughter. Soon they found an open area.

The boys backed away from each other so their lines wouldn't get tangled. Then they grabbed their kites in one hand and their spools in the other.

"Ready?" yelled Dudley.

Henry nodded. Then both

An excerpt from *Henry Heckelbeck and the Race Car Derby*